i

The

Malevolence

of

Annie Mae

*****

Christopher B. Howell

For permission request, write to the author, addressed:
Christopher B. Howell
3519 Firestone Drive
Charlotte N.C 28216

ACKNOWLEDGMENTS

 I would like to thank God for giving me the courage to write this book. Secondly, I would like to thank my mother Overseer B.C Howell for raising and keeping me in the church. I appreciate the constructive criticism and unconditional love you have given me over the years. Thirdly, I would like to thank my dad, Cornelius Howell Jr. for being a great father, role model and inspiration in my life. I appreciate the great advice you have given me throughout the years. Also, thanks for standing strong whenever times got hard. Finally, I like to thank all my friends and family members for their continuing support.

Thanks!!!

In memory of my grandmother:

Overseer Dollie E. Huey

Luke 9:62

But Jesus said to him, "No one, having put his hand to the plow, and looking back, is fit for the kingdom of God."

Introduction

*****

    I've been going to church ever since I can remember. That's because my momma, "Sarah S. Richardson" would make me go every Sunday. We would leave out around eight thirty in the morning and usually didn't get home until around eleven o'clock at night. We stayed in church all day on Sundays and had to go back again on Wednesday nights for Bible study. I didn't get a chance to enjoy my summer months because I had to attend vacation Bible school as well. As a kid, I didn't get a chance to enjoy the summertime activities like my friends, so I had plenty of leisure time to sit back and judge the members of the church.

Going to church every week allowed me to see just how fake church folks could be, especially when they call themselves the "Saints of God". They attend church every Sunday and testify on the goodness of God and then turn around, and act like devils throughout the week. They have no regards for those who helped pave the way for them to praise God. See, my grandmother was a patriot for the community and put in countless hours of headaches and turmoil during the Jim Crow era. She used to set up demonstrations and protests so that these hypocrites could drink from the same water fountains as the white folks. Some of them hide in the church for sanctuary, while others seem to think that their tithes and offering gives them a free ticket to heaven. They give all their hard-earned money to the church, while the preachers live a lavish lifestyle.

My name is Steve Richardson, and these are just a few of the issues that I had to deal with as a child. It took me several years to acknowledge and to admit that I have anger issues, because I struggle daily. So, to remain calm, I have to say this prayer:

"God please, grant me the serenity to accept the things I cannot change, Courage to change the things I can, and wisdom to know the difference."

"Reinhold Niebuhr"

The Malevolence of Annie Mae

Proverbs 22:6

" Train up a child in the way he should go,

And when he is old, he will not depart from it"

Chapter 1

*****

Sunday, July 21, 1985

It was a Sunday morning, and as usual, you could smell the aroma from Momma's cooking miles away. The smell was like a fragrant alarm clock that woke me up and reminded me exactly what day of the week it was. Momma was getting ready for church and had to leave early because it was the bishop's 6th anniversary, and her week to usher. The church we attend is called: First Revival Pentecostal Church, under the Leadership of Bishop CW Smith Jr.

I hope to never set foot in there again because they have about four hundred and fifty members and most of them are hypocrites just playing church. Bishop CW Smith Jr. is the son of the late CW Smith, the founding father of the church which he started in the early '50s.

He was known around town as being "The ladies' man." The rumor has it that he has a bunch of kids spread throughout the surrounding Counties. He was like King David and never slowed down with the women until the day he died. He took his last breath in the bed at the home of one of his parishioners and when questioned, she told everyone that she was being delivered: which was the reason for the 2 a.m. visit.

Bishop CW Smith Jr., the current Pastor of the church, is a slender, well-groomed man who walks, talks, and looks just like a hustler. He was once a pimp in Dallas, Texas, before moving back to Haney County. When he first came to town, he always had beautiful ladies on his side and wore custom tailored suits and alligator-skinned shoes. He came to town, driving a 1973 convertible Cadillac Eldorado with gangster whitewall tires and custom rims. This car was a one-of-a-kind Caddy that had a statue of Jesus hanging on the cross as a hood ornament. He has since then, replaced his convertible Caddy and upgraded it to a new two door Bentley, courtesy of the church's tithes and offerings.

In Houston Texas, he was known as the Preaching Pimp, because he used to quote Bible scriptures while collecting his money. If any "hoe" they called them, came up short on their cash for the night, he would put baby powder on his hand before smacking them with a pimp's over-hand slap. I thought it was funny when I first heard the story and didn't believe it until I remembered when Miss Johnson went up for prayer. She started shouting and accidentally stepped on his alligator-skinned shoes. He gave her a stare, looked down at his shoes, and slapped the false teeth out of her mouth and her wig flew off. You could see the imprint from his hand on her face. He tried to play it off by saying that Miss Johnson had a demonic spirit. She had to be at least 80 years old at the time. God rest her soul.

 The First Lady of the church name is Veronica Smith. Veronica is a light-skinned lady with a huge ego and a very big mouth. When she talks, you need a dictionary to understand her words. She always uses sophisticated words that no one ever knows what it means. I heard her tell Miss Jones one day. "The church's parishioners will not allow your impertinent attitude to desecrate the house of the lord."

 I overheard a few women gossiping about her and one of them said: "Just because she has a college Degree, she thinks she so dignified. She ain't nothing but one of Bishop's high-class hoes."

What I do know for sure is that she is very bossy and controlling. Sometimes it's hard to tell who's running the church.

She is said to be fooling around with the head deacon of the church, Dexter Alexander. Deacon Alexander is muscular and very athletic looking. He stands about 6'6" and weighs in at a solid 250 lbs. He loves to attract attention because he always wears tight suits and T-shirts under his dress coat. Whenever he takes up the offering, he always takes off his jacket and moves his chest muscles from left to right. I remember one time a lady was looking so hard, that she missed the entire offering plate.

 Now, whenever it comes to the offering; the church takes up about five different ones: the tithes & offering, the musician and choir fund, the missionary board fund, the choir anniversary fund, and one for the building fund.

They have been taking up money for the building fund for years, and the church still looks run down and in need of work. There have been recent talks about buying a new church, but the only thing that has been new over the years is the bishops' house, cars, and expensive taste in clothes. I can't understand why momma still insist on going to church every single week, when she can barely afford to pay the light bill.

The last time I went to church, they were having devotional prayer, and my friends and I were playing a card game called "tonk." While the church members were in a deep consecrated prayer; Paul dropped his cards and tonked out, thinking he had the better hand. I slammed the cards on the pew and yelled, "Tonk... fool!"

You should have seen the faces of the church members as they all lifted their heads. That's when the Bishop jumped up, and he and the mothers of the church came to the back pew with a bottle of anointing oil and began to openly rebuke us. The Bishop kept shouting, "In the name of Jesus, In the name of Jesus. Satan, I rebuke "thee" in the name of Jesus!"

It was funny because Paul began to act as if he was having a seizure and started speaking in fake tongues. My other two friends and I, Keith, and Bobby joined in and started faking too; like we were on fire and filled with the Spirit. We started shouting and running around the church with our hands in the air hollering and repeating Jesus. Everyone thought we were tarrying for the Holy

Ghost, but my Momma knew that we were faking, and she was so embarrassed. That was the last time she made me go to church.

"Steve!" she yelled. "Hurry up and eat your breakfast before it gets cold, you know I have to be at church early! It's Pastor's anniversary, and I don't want to be late."

"You mean your Pastor's anniversary," I mumbled under my breath.

I proceeded slowly and made my way to the kitchen table.

"Why are you still going to that church anyway?" I asked.

In her slave voice, she continued.

"Where else can I go, I know you don't want me going to church with them white folks. You know they don't care for us colored people?

Besides, the only other church to go to is across the river, and you know those folks are too dignified! When the spirit hits me, I like to get my shout on."

She began shouting in emphasis as we both begin to laugh.

As Momma continued to prepare my food, I wondered what I'd do if something were to ever happen to her. I know she was joking about going across the river, but I noticed that she would always look down every time there's a mention, and you could hear the pitch of her voice change. I could always tell if she had something on her mind or if she was troubled in her spirit. She would always quote her favorite scripture.

Psalm 46:1-2

"God is our refuge and strength, a very present help in trouble. Therefore, will not we fear, though the earth be removed, and though the mountains be carried into the midst of the sea."

The talk of going across the river is the only time she lacks faith and doesn't practice what she preaches.

Across the river is only twenty miles away and located in a little town called Jonesville.

Jonesville is a small town in Murray County with a population of fewer than three thousand people. To get there it takes about forty-five minutes, but you can make it in less than fifteen if you take the shortcut through Deadman's Curve.

Deadman's Curve is on the south end of Haney County, and it is extremely dark and foggy at night. It has been rumored that Deadman's Curve has a female ghost dressed in all black that comes out and lurks the area to find her lost husband. They say as you approach the Curve, you can see her face through your rearview mirror sitting in the back seat, and just as you attempt to hit the Curve; she suddenly reappears in the middle of the foggy road. I believe this is the reason she never likes taking the shortcut to Jonesville to see her longtime friend, Deacon Jones.

James Jones, also known as, Deacon JJ, is a tall militant man who always looks nervous and jumpy. I heard that he was once a Sergeant Major in the United States Army a few years back, and I believe he's shell-shocked from his time served in the military. He has a gash on his forehead, very dark-skinned, and so black that I once thought he came straight from the jungles of Africa. He has glossy eyes that make him look very scary. I asked momma why his eyes look that way, and she said it was because of a condition called "cataract."

Deacon JJ grew up in Jonesville and he and Momma have been friends for years. I heard that he owns a funeral home and used to be a heavy smoker, gambler, and an alcoholic a few years back. He's a creepy looking guy and I caught him staring at me at Church on several occasions over the years. I wanted to say something to Momma, but I knew she wouldn't believe me since she already knows I don't like him.

"Steve!" she yelled. "Boy, I've been calling your name for almost two minutes. Open those ears of yours and stop daydreaming so much! You and them bad friends need to come and hear God's word."

"Ma, my friends are not bad, they're just like me."

"Like what?" she asked.

"They're misunderstood."

"Misunderstood my foot, whenever you get with them boys, I know y'all be up to no good."

"Ma, you always think we up to something; at least they have a daddy in the house."

Right then, I could see that I struck a nerve. I could tell by her facial expression that she was agitated.

"Boy..., You can't steal my joy. The devil is a liar!" she yelled.

"Momma, I'm not trying to steal your joy, but it's the truth. You never want to talk about my daddy."

Right then and there she ignored me, like she always does whenever I bring up the subject.

"Make sure you clean these dishes and your nasty room.

Cleanliness is next to Godliness," she stated.

"Yes ma'am," I replied as I pouted.

"I'll see you when I get back, and I love you!" She said.

I dropped my head as I shied away.

This was my opportunity to let my mother know just how much I loved her, but there was something inside of me that wouldn't let me say it. It could have been the boy that never grew up without a father, or maybe me just trying to be tough. Whatever it was, just wouldn't let me say those three simple words.

"See you after church," she said as she walked out of the door.

At that moment, I started feeling bad for not letting her know just how much I loved her; but upset because she never talks about my dad. I feel like I'm the only kid in Haney that grew up without a father.

My last memory of him is when he came home drunk and upset after supposedly losing all the bill money on a poker game in Jonesville. That argument between him and momma is the last thing I remember.

That was over ten years ago.

It was once rumored that he used the poker game as an excuse to run around on momma with his side chick. I wish I knew the truth; maybe it would help ease some of this anger that I have on the inside. It really hurts, not knowing much about him and always wondering if the rumors are true. I remember his name "John Richardson," and he was born in a little town in South Carolina called Matthews. He had no other living relatives that I know of, and I was his only kid. I was told that he met momma at the State Fair, and they married three weeks later. They had what you called a "shotgun wedding." At the time, I didn't know what it meant, but momma was fifteen years old, and he was twenty-one.

I overheard Miss Johnson say that my dad likes to rock the cradle. After understanding what the phrase meant, I realized that he could have gone to jail for getting her pregnant so young. I don't have any of his pictures because momma burnt them along with his clothes on the front yard about two days after he didn't come home. I remember she would cry and then lock herself in her room for hours after he would leave the house. I will never forget that rainy night because that was the last time I ever saw him alive.

Momma finally made it off to church, and just like every Sunday, I met the boys down by the lake at our favorite fishing spot. We usually meet there every Sunday around noon to fish and plan devious events during the summer weeks. This week was my turn to come up with something that we could all sit back, laugh, and talk about for weeks. I went to the utility closet and grabbed my fishing clothes that were in a black bag. This is the bag that momma knew about, but I kept hid from her because I was too lazy to wash them myself. She started making me put my fishing clothes there because she didn't want the smell to get in her clothes whenever she washed.

The time was 11:20 a.m., and I knew that if I didn't get to the secret fishing spot in time, one of the boys would get a head start on trying to win our weekly bet of catching the biggest fish. I hopped on my bike and headed for the lake.

****

I finally made it to the lake and realized that Keith was already there. Keith is my best friend, the oldest and the competitive one. He's the one who usually engineers most of our projects, and the one who feels he is right about everything.

His family is wealthy, and they stay in an all-brick two-story home. Although his dad is the County's' doctor, and his mother is the town's only female lawyer, he isn't the smartest. Both of his parents are also members of First Revival. His mother is the church treasurer, and his dad is on the board of trustees. If you could buy your way into heaven, they would be the first ones to do so.

"Dang…. man!" I shouted.

Keith started laughing. "The early bird gets the worm!" he countered.

"What time did you get here?" I asked.

About twenty-five minutes ago. "I wanted to try out my secret bait". he replied.

"What secret bait?" I inquired.

"Now…, if I tell you, it wouldn't be a secret," he stated as he smiled.

"I don't care what you use; I'm still going to be the first to catch bubba!" I shouted.

Just as we were going back and forth with words, Paul and Bobby arrived.

Paul and Bobby are cousins, and they are also my childhood friends. Paul is the chubby one and the class clown of the group. He is also the smartest of my friends. Both of his parents are teachers at the local school and are very devout Christians. His mother is our Sunday school teacher, and his daddy's one of the deacons at the church. Bobby is only thirteen and the youngest in the bunch. He's the shy and timid one in our group. His dad works at the local factory, and his mother is a stay-at-home mom, who takes care of him and his four siblings. Bobby's' dad was once a trusted member at First Revival. He would faithfully pay his tithes and offerings to the church. Whenever he was laid off at his job and had no income, the church wouldn't lend him the money to stop his house from foreclosure. That's why he and his family stopped going to church a few years back.

 I thought it was wrong for the church not to help considering the Bishop and his wife stays in a neighborhood surrounded by white folks.

"What in the heck y'all arguing about this week?" Paul asked.

"Them' five dollars y'all going to be coughing up when I catch 'Big Bubba'" I said.

"Boy, you ain't catching nothing, when those fish get a whip of my new bait, they're going to be mine!" Keith shouted.

"What new bait?" Bobby asked.

"It's a secret," I stated.

Just as we were talking, there was an awful smell that swept the air. We all yelled in unison.

"Whew..., What in the heck is that smell"?

"It's the secret bait I was telling y'all about. Chitterlings," Keith said.

"Secret my foot, them chitterlings smells like pure booty juice," Paul stated.

"Nah, they smell like Deacon Smith's breath," I added.

We all started laughing, but I noticed that Bobby remained silent.

"Bobby! What's wrong with you?" I asked.

"Nothing," he slowly replied.

"He's been silent for a minute," Paul said.

"Are you OK?" I asked.

"My mom and dad have been fighting again, and I think it's serious this time, because he left the house."

"Now Bob, you know Uncle Raymond always leaves the house after arguing with your momma, but you know, he'll come back eventually. Cheer up!" Paul said.

"Yeah, cheer up before I put these chitlins in your mouth," I said.

We all grabbed some of Keith's chitterling baits from his cooler and started chasing each other around the lake.

After about fifteen minutes of throwing chitterlings and running around, we all laid by the bank of the lake, fully exhausted.

"Hey Steve, whose week is it to pick out the plan for this summer?" Keith asked.

"It's my turn," I said.

"Well, have you thought of anything for us to do?" he asked.

"Yeah, I'm tired of egging cars, throwing toilet tissue into trees, and ringing people's doorbells. We need something that whenever school starts, we can talk about all year," Paul said.

"Well, I haven't given it much thought, it seems like we've done just about everything we could do. Besides, it's going to be hard to top the time when Bobby put a bottle of laxative in Mother Smith's signature spaghetti," I explained.

"Oh boy! I remember that, and Paul went and hid all the toilet tissue in the church," Keith added.

"Yeah, I said, that was during last year's church anniversary. Man, those church folks were afraid to shout and praise God. When Bishop saw that his preaching moved no one, he got angry and started slapping people upside the head with anointing oil."

"Yeah, and he started getting the laxative stomach cramps and almost doo-dooed in his brand-new robe," Bobby added.

"Yeah, he ran to the toilet faster than Carl Lewis in last year's summer Olympics," I said.

We all laughed.

"What about the time when Keith put chlorine tablets in the baptism pool just before Sister Jones got baptized. It burnt her hair and scalp. She came up and started fanning her head and screaming, and people thought she caught the Holy Ghost!

Her scalp was on fire," Paul said, laughing.

"Yeah, we had some good laughs over the years, but we need something different this time so that we can someday tell our kids," Keith said.

"So, what do you have in mind Steve?" Paul asked.

"Well, do y'all remember the mannequin in the utility closet in the art & science building? The one that everybody calls Annie?" I said.

"Yeah, the creepy looking one that always stares at you, and people swear that it comes to life at night," Keith replied.

"Yeah" I said. " All we need to do is dress her up like a real person and stand her up to scare people. We just have to find a way to make it all look real."

"That's a great idea Steve; she already looks real anyway." Keith said.

"That mannequin is real. I remember the time when Mr. Peel asked me to get some supplies out of the utility room, and when I went inside the closet; I heard that mannequin say, "Get out."

Shoo, I ran so fast, I forgot what the heck I was looking for," Paul stated in a frightened voice.

"Man stop lying, you know good and well, your fat butt ain't ran nowhere," Keith chided.

"Yeah, nowhere but to the store to get some "Chico sticks," I said.

"Y'all always think someone be lying'," he retorted.

"Because you do! You're always trying to scare somebody!" shouted Bobby.

At this time, Paul pulled his shirt over his head and started walking towards Bobby with his hands and arms out like a zombie. He started moaning, "Oh Bobby, Oh Bobby, I'm going to get you."

Bobby started running and shouted back, "Man! You play too much!

We all started laughing and shaking as if we were frightened.

After about ten minutes of running around, Keith asked the question.

"Hey Steve, how are we supposed to get the mannequin from the art building and take it to Deadman's Curve?"

"I already got it figured out. Three weeks from now on August 16th, the Church has its annual women's convention." James and my momma always carpool that week. That's one of the biggest events of the year because Bishop TC Collins always preaches an eight-day revival. It starts that Friday and won't end until the 24th of the following week.

"What does that have to do with anything Steve?" Paul replied.

"James usually picks up momma for Church in his car. We can drive my momma's car that Saturday and take Annie to Deadman's Curve. Y'all can meet me at my house, and we can all ride together."

"How do we supposed to get into the school?" asked Bobby.

"Bobby…, You are acting like you ride the short bus. We're going to break in like we always do!" Paul shouted.

" They will never know Annie is missing; she's been in the utility closet for years," I said.

Just as we were talking, Keith's fishing line started to move. He grabbed his fishing pole and began to tug on it out of excitement.

"I told y'all my secret bait was the bomb," He yelled.

He started tussling to reel it in. I ran over and grabbed my net and rushed into the water to help retrieve the big catch. I grabbed his line and dipped my net into the cold muddy water.

"Wow," I shouted out of excitement.

After years of being a legendary myth, big bubba has finally met his sudden demise.

You caught a big one Keith; them chitterlings of yours sure lived up to its expectation.

You just caught a twenty-five-pound work boot."   I shouted.

We all laughed until tears ran down our faces.

Twenty minutes had passed.

"Well fellas, it looks like nobody's going to win the bet this week. Let's all meet back up next week so that we can go over more details," I said.

"Make sure you can get your mom's car. We don't need any mistakes." Keith said.

"I got this, I'm a hook Annie up!" I explained.

"Well Steve, don't have Annie looking like she on the usher board, with the white stockings and open toe shoes like your momma. Her toenails be coming out of her stocking and overlapping the shoes," Paul teased.

"That's okay Paul, it's still better than your momma, because your momma so fat, when she wears stockings and fart, her ankle swells," I said jokingly.

We all laughed.

"What time is it?" asked Bobby.

"Time for you to get a watch," Keith responded with a grin.

"For real man, stop playing."

"It's 2:45 pm. Why?" he asked.

"Ah.... man, I suppose to be cutting the grass," he shouted.

"Dang...., and I suppose to be doing my chores. My momma's going to kill me. I'll see y'all tomorrow." I said.

I grabbed my fishing rod and rushed home as fast as I could.

 As I approached the house, I noticed that momma was already home.

I dropped my bike and gear and crept around to the backyard. I tried to sneak in through my bedroom window, but it was locked. I thought to myself, now, I know I left it open because I always do. Then just when I was about to turn around, I heard a loud shout,

"Steve!"

"I thought I told you to clean up this house before I left!" momma yelled.

I hurried and ran into the house as she held the back door open.

"I work too doggone hard to be putting up with a hard-headed chap. Just because you fifteen, don't mean I won't whip your behind."

I knew by the sound of her voice, her frustration wasn't geared towards me, but something that happened at church. I just had to wait to find out what was really bothering her.

"Momma, I'm sorry,"

Once, I said sorry, she seemed to get even madder.

"Sorry huh!" she chided.

Right then and there, I started mimicking her word for word because I've heard them a thousand times.

"Boy..., I carried you for nine months, fed you, and put food on this table and you sitting here acting like you don't appreciate nothing I do."

Right then and there, I knew the words that would comfort her and keep her calm.

I whispered,

"Please forgive me?"

It was just that moment, and as always, those words found a way to comfort her. I waited for a few minutes for her to cool down and then asked.

"How was Church today?"
 "That Bishop is working my nerves. Every time I turn around, he always needing money. He needs money for this and always needs money for that," she said.

"Didn't y'all just buy him a Bentley?" I asked.

"Yeah, and a new robe. Now, he says that he's been praying to God for a new fur coat. Talking about he needs two thousand dollars. He just wants to show off that coat whenever Bishop TC Collins comes to town in a few weeks," she said.
It's going to be too hot and over 100-degrees in the church. He's going to burn up in the pulpit." I said.
"Remember at last year's Convention, he had on a pink one and it didn't seem to bother him then," Momma said.
"Yeah, I remember because he had on the matching fur hat to go with the coat. He looked like an Easter bunny sitting in the pulpit."
"That's not nice" she said.
We both just laughed.

"I'm telling you; you can't even use the bathroom in the church because of the floor sinking. Now he over here talking about a two-thousand-dollar fur coat! It seems like every week; he wants all my little bit of money. I'm on a fixed income." She sighed.

"Well momma, the Bible did say over in Malachi for you to bring all the tithes and offering into the storehouse, that there may be meat in the Bishops house," I quoted.

"Boy, hush up and stop miss-quoting scriptures and get a job, so you can start helping out with some of these bills," she said.

"You mean the house bills or the Bishop's bills?" I retorted.

We both laughed.

"Boy, go ahead and do your chores and clean up that room. Make sure you wash those nasty clothes in that bag too. You thought I didn't know huh?" She said with a smirk on her face.

"No Ma, I didn't think that. You said you didn't want to get that fishy smell in your clothes."

"Steve, you're getting too old for me to be running behind you and telling you what you suppose to do. You're almost 16 years old, and it's time for you to start being a man."

"Momma, I have another two months before that happen, but until then, I just want to enjoy being a kid."

"Boy, you just like your daddy," she whispered.

"Huh ma, what you say?" I asked.

"Never mind, just go do your chores like I asked you to," she said as she left the room.

Ephesians 4:26

" Be angry, and do not sin": do not let the sun go down on your wrath"

Chapter 2

✳✳✳✳✳

Monday, July 22, 1985

It was Monday around 7 a.m., and momma wanted to let me know that she was headed to work. "Steve," she said, "did you wash those dishes like I asked you to?"

"Yes ma'am," I said in my sleepy voice.

"Well, it doesn't look like you did. I want you to rewash them, and if they're not clean when I get back home; I'm a make you clean them again. Anything worth doing is worth doing right the first time," she said.

"Okay Ma, I will."

"I Love you," she shouted.

I paused for a minute, and again, I just couldn't seem to tell her those three simple words.

Momma has two jobs, the first is at the local mill as a janitor. She's been working there for years and her second job she helps cleans the owners home part-time on Monday and Wednesdays.

The company where she works is called Haney's Cotton Mill, and has been in business since 1866, almost a year after slavery. It was said that Mr. Murray Haney, the original owner, was part of the KKK and had black folks picking cotton on free labor, even after the emancipation. People don't know it, but momma once told me that she was cleaning up John Haney, the great grandson's house, and she found a clansman suit in his closet. The Haney's own just about every business in Haney, Murray, and Waynesville County, so momma said it would be best to keep it a secret.

That was over five years ago.

I couldn't go back to sleep after momma woke me up, so I went into the kitchen and fixed me some leftovers that she had cooked two days prior. She brought me a plate from church yesterday, but when I saw a dead roach in my food the last time; I stopped eating food from the church.

"Steve," I heard a voice coming from outside.

"Open the door fool, it's me, Keith."

"Why are you up so early," I asked.

"I came to give you a message."

"Do you remember Suzie Jenkins?" he asked.

"You mean, Suzie with the cross eyes?" I replied.

"Yeah, cross-eyed Suzie. I ran into her at the Murray food Mart, and she asked about you, she said that you were the apple of her eye," Keith chuckled.

"Well, she must a saw two apples then, because the last time we saw her at the State Fair, I couldn't tell if she was looking at me or looking at you. Her eyeballs look huge in those thick glasses.

Nobody's going to catch me courting no four-eyed fool. She ain't messing up my rep'," I said.

"Man, you lame, you don't have a rep,"

"What's for lunch he asked?"

"Some leftovers my momma cooked a couple of days ago. Why, do you want some?" I asked.

"Yeah, what you got?"

"I got some chicken feet over rice and gravy, pinto beans, collards, and some cornbread." I explained.

"You eat chicken feet, "yuck," I can't believe you eating them nasty thangs!"

"Yeah, they good too, all you have to do is put them in your mouth and start sucking the toes." I sucked the toes of the chicken to demonstrate.

"Man, you are nasty. My daddy said that when black folks eat like that, they get the sugar diabase'," he said.

"You mean sugar diabetes dummy. My momma don't put no sugar in her chicken feet," I corrected.

We both started laughing.

"Steve, what did you mean yesterday when you said you were going to hook Annie up. What are you planning on doing?" he asked.

"Do you remember the black dress on display in the window at the Fashion Mart?"

"Yeah, I remember. It's the same one all the ladies in town were talking about. My momma wanted that dress," he said.

"Well, I saved up all my money last summer and bought her that dress for her birthday."

"I wonder who bought the other dress because I heard my mom tell Mrs. Jones that they had two in stock." He said.

"It was James. He bought the other dress. My momma didn't want to hurt our feelings, so she kept them both."

"Man, that's messed up," he replied.

"Yeah, I know, so now my momma calls both of them her favorite dress. I figured that if I took one and used it to dress Annie, she wouldn't miss it."

"Well, as much as that dress cost, you better hope she doesn't!" Keith replied.

"Yeah, I know," I said with a smirk on my face.

"Keith," I asked. "What are we doing today?"

"I don't know, but let's go over to Paul's house and see what we can get into."

We hopped on our bikes and headed towards Paul's house. Paul's house was only a twenty-minute bike ride from mine, but I dread going there. His folks are English teachers, and they are always trying to correct our grammar. Keith changes his voice whenever he gets around them. I guess it's because they know that his daddy is a doctor, and mother is an attorney.

We jumped off our bikes and headed for the front door. I rang the doorbell, and his dad answered the door; he was in a robe and had a cigar pipe in his mouth.

He said in a distinct voice.

"Hello gentlemen, how may I help you?"

Keith immediately responded in an English accent by saying, "Fine sir, can Paul come out and play?"

He disguised his voice to sound like an Englishman. I made sure I kept quiet because I didn't feel like being corrected. Keith did all the talking, and I swear I thought he was from England at one point. For someone who didn't know how to pronounce diabetes; he sure got eloquent with his words.

Paul finally came out of the house.

"Man, I ain't never been so glad to see you," I shouted.

Keith corrected me by saying in his proper English accent: "You should have said, I have never been so glad to see you."

"You're a fake. You always put on a front when we get around Paul's folks, up here trying to sound like Oliver Twist," I chided.

"I have to represent." He said.

"Represent my foot, your grammar is worse than mine."

"You should have been the one to play Othello in the school play. You're faker than a three-dollar bill."

Keith started prancing and waving his hands in motions of enchantments as he said in his fake English accent, "Romeo, Romeo, Where art thou Romeo."

Paul shouted, "That's not Othello dummy! That's Romeo and Juliet."

"See…, that's what I'm talking about. I told you he was fake; he probably doesn't even know who Shakespeare is!"

We all started laughing.

"Hey Paul," said Keith. "Where is Bobby, did his dad come home last night?"

"I think so, he had to go to work this morning. That man's not missing out on his money; he got too many mouths to feed," Paul said.

"I can't see how his daddy put up with that woman's mouth. Every time you turn around, she always fussing about something.

The Bible says over in Proverbs 21:9, 25:24 and 21:19

"It's better to be on a rooftop by yourself than to be in a house with a woman who be running her mouth all the time," I paraphrased.

"Look at the Reverend." Keith taunted.

"I'm serious, it was so important that Solomon had to write it down three times, and the book of Ecclesiasticus 25:16 has its own version.

"Who taught you that?" Paul asked.

"Your momma dummy, isn't she the Sunday school teacher? Your folks need to stop correcting people's grammar and start teaching you about the word of God!" I said.

We all laughed.

We rode our bikes down to Haney's Market because Paul wanted some Chico sticks. I really didn't want to go, because I didn't care to much for the store clerk, Mrs. Mae.

*****

We made it to Haney's.

"I'm staying outside," I said.

"What are you scared of?" Paul asked.

"I'm not scared. I just don't want Mrs. Mae sweating me. I don't have to steal, because my momma gives me ten dollars a week for doing chores around the house," I said.

"Good, because I'm a need them dollars for my Chico sticks", Paul stated.

We all went in and immediately Mrs. Mae's eyes were glued in on us. She followed us and began peeking in between the aisles. She watched us until we got up to the register.

Paul shouted, "Steve, I change my mind. I want a pickled pig feet and some Jungle Juice.

"You trying to spend all my money," I pouted.

When we got up to the counter, Mrs. Mae yelled, "I hope y'all boys ain't got nothing hidden in them pockets; you know what they do to black folks in the prisons!

"No ma'am," Paul said.

"You boys are going to end up on the chain gang," she said.

At this time, I became furious and upset at Keith and Paul for kissing up to Mrs. Mae. I'm sick and tired of her always being so judgmental.

She acts just like a "House negro."

"HOW MUCH DO I OWE YOU?!" I shouted.

"Boy, you shouldn't be raising your voice to grown folks. If you had a father in the home, you wouldn't be so disrespectful. That's a shame what happened to him anyways. At least he had good enough sense not to be disrespectful to grown folks!" she scorned.

With my lip poked out and arms folded, I shouted, "You don't know anything about my daddy!"

"Boy…, you have a lot to learn. That'll be three dollars and fifty cents," she said as she shook her head.

I pulled out a book of food stamps to pay my bill and Paul and Keith began laughing in the background. I was curious about what Mrs. Mae had just said, so I ignored them for the moment. My pride wouldn't let me ask her what she meant, yet I was curious. I received my change and walked outside.

Keith and Paul were still laughing and joking with me about the food stamps.

"Man…, I thought you had some real money. I didn't know you had food stamps," Paul said jokingly.

"Yeah, he pulled them Food stamps out like he was a baller," Keith laughed.

"Y'all think everything is so doggone funny!"

I hopped on my bike and rode off angry.

Keith and Paul were yelling out loud,

"What's wrong? We were just playing!"

I rode off and ignored them because my anger began to intensify. I kept hearing Mrs. Mae's voice again playing over and over in my head. That was the third time I'd heard people say things about my daddy.

The first time was when I overheard the ushers gossiping and talking about how nice my father looked. One of them said that looking at him made it easy on the eyes.

The second time was when I almost got suspended from school for fighting. Mr. Blackwell our Guidance school Counselor; sat me down and counseled me about my anger. The school called it anger management classes. He told me that I needed to learn how to control my anger. Coincidentally, the same thing granny use to say. She said that my temper reminded her of someone. I thought she was talking about my daddy for all these years, but I realized that it was my momma the whole time.

My Granny use to tell me to never let the sun go down on my wrath.

At the time, I was too young to understand what she meant and I'm sure she told my momma the same thing. I often wonder if she ever felt bad for arguing with my father that night. My Granny taught us both, that anytime another person can bring you out of character; that person has dominion and power to control your life. My granny was a very wise lady, and she was the only person who could keep us calm.

1 Chronicles 16:22

"Touch not mine anointed and do my prophets no harm.".

Chapter 3

✶✶✶✶✶

August 4, 1985

It was Sunday, August 4th, and I managed to ignore my friends for almost two weeks. I realized that my anger came from being embarrassed by Mrs. Mae; and for that reason, I sometimes envy my friends for having a father in the home.

Steve!" Momma called. "What's going on with you?"

"Nothing," I said.

"Well, it's not like you to be cooped up in the house," she said.

"There's nothing wrong Ma, I just don't feel like being bothered.

"Well, I was making sure that you were okay. Guess who I ran into at church last week," she asked.

"Let me guess…. Jesus?" I joked.

"Boy, stop trying to be funny. I saw Suzie Jenkins, and she asked about you. She wanted to know if you were working at the County's Inaugural Ball in October. I told her you were, and that you were really looking forward to seeing her."

"Ma, how can you sign me up for something I didn't even know about? Besides, you didn't even ask me if I wanted to work."

"Ask you for what, you know Mr. Haney is running for the Governor's seat, and me and James both have to be there to serve the guest."

"James, why does he have to be there?" I said.

"The same reason why you're going to be there; to make some money. I asked Mrs. Haney if you could work, and she said that she could use an extra buss-boy."

"Ma, I'm not going to be in the mood to be serving them old high-class white folks; let alone, be working alongside somebody I don't even like."

"Well, I never asked you who you liked or not. Besides, I already told Mrs. Haney that you would work. This job will keep you busy and even help put money in your pocket for the prom. You might even have enough money left over to buy that new fishing rod you been talking about."

"Maaaa...," I moaned.

"Ma, nothing! It's all said and done. You're going to be there and that's it!" she said in her stern voice.

"Yes ma'am," I replied.

"This event is very important to the Haney's, and lord knows I need my job. It will be nice to see you and Suzie working together. That's the kind of girl you ought to be taking to the prom; she seems like a respectable young lady. She looks like she has some good home training too," Momma said.

"Just because her daddy works at the bank doesn't mean she has good home training," I said.

"Well, she looks a lot better than that "hussy" you took to the ninth grade Prom last year."

"You mean Monica?" I shouted.

"Yeah, the one with two kids already, and she just turned 16," she said.

At this time, I wanted to quote Matthew 7:1-2 and remind her how old she was when she had me; but I kept quiet. Granny always told me that I should always learn when to choose my battles, and this surely wasn't the time.

"Momma, what's going on at church today?" I asked.

"The church is supposed to be giving Bishop the fur coat he claimed he'd been praying about."

"Why does he need a fur coat in the summer, its 98 degrees outside?" I asked.

"I already told you; he just wants to put on a show next week for Bishop TC Collins. You remember, he's coming to our church next week," she said.

"Yeah... I know, he's the talk of the town," I replied.

"That man sure can preach, He has that anointing that can break any yoke!" she stated as she threw her hands up towards heaven.

"He scares me," I said.

"Why, because he be prophesying?" she said.

"Nah..., because he be prophe-lying. He tells folks just what they want to hear, and they be steadily bringing him money. He's phony just like Bishop Smith," I said.

"There you go again; you don't suppose to spread discord on a man of God, that's an abomination."

The Bible says in 1st Chronicles 16:22

"Do not touch my anointed ones and do my prophets no harm." She quoted.

"Well..., he told me that God was going to answer my Prayer, and it hasn't happened yet," I said.

"No Steve, Bishop told you that over in

Luke 8:17

'For nothing is secret that will not be revealed, nor anything hidden that will not be known and come to light.'

"He told you that God has sheltered you all these years for a reason and that he would reveal the things you been praying for in due time. He told you to be steadfast and let God fight your battles. I remember just like it was yesterday because I felt the spirit of God moving in the church that night.

Momma began raising her hands in the air and started shouting and chanting "Halleluiah. "

"Well, I don't know what you felt that night, because all I felt was the lint in my back pocket. By the time I sat down, all my money was gone. It took me the whole summer to make forty dollars, and less than thirty minutes to lose it that same night."

"I have never seen Bishop TC Collins take up money for using his gift," she declared.

"Yeah…, I know because he charges $40 for those prayer cloths!"

We both laughed.

"Hey ma, Is James still going to pick you up for the convention?"

"Boy, what kind of question is that? You know next week is the women's time to be serenaded and pampered. Why…., are you coming to support your Momma?" she asked.

"No……, it's because I'm trying to stay far away from TC Collins as possible." I said.

"Why, are you afraid he's going to tell you something you don't want to hear?" she giggled.

"Nah…, it's because I don't have another $40 for a prayer cloth!"

We both laughed.

"Boy, you're going to make me late for church fooling around with you. I left you a plate on the stove. Please make sure you clean up behind yourself. "I Love you!" she yelled as she rushed out the door.

The time was around 11:45 am, and I knew that the boys were on their way to the lake. I put on my fishing clothes, grabbed my gear, and headed towards that direction.

As I got closer, I heard Paul shout,

"Hey Steve, we sure missed you!"

"Yeah, we sure did, you must have been in hibernation," Bobby added.

"Nah... I'm good, I just had a few things on my mind."

"Well, it looks like you owe Keith five dollars; he caught "Big Bubba" last week," he replied.

"He caught him with them stinking chitterlings too!" Paul added.

"FOR REAL??" I shouted.

"Yeah..., I want my money in cash; not in food stamps either," Keith quipped.

We all laughed.

"I'm sorry for ignoring y'all, but Mrs. Mae had me going."

"Well..., we need you to be focused for next week," said Paul.

"I'm focused. My Momma already assured me that James is picking her up. You just make sure you're at my house around 6:30 " I said.

"OK…, but make sure you don't forget about that dress you were talking about," said Keith.

"Of course, I've already picked out the outfit for Annie. I'm going to be dressing her up in a black dress, boots, and my granny's black veil to match," I replied.

"Let's pick Annie up on Friday night and start a day earlier," Bobby said.

"Nah…, that's not a good idea because I told my daddy, I was coming to church that night. He wants me to be there and show support for my momma," Paul said.

"Man…, I can't believe you're going to church. Bishop TC Collin's is going to prophesize to you just like he did Steve last year." Keith said.

Yeah, I remember; that dude is creepy looking. Bobby added.

Well, you don't have to worry about me, I already told my momma that I wasn't going," I said.

Well, I'm not scared of no prophet and besides, he has never prophesized to me. I'm just going to show my support," Paul said.

Well, good luck because I'm not going. Just make sure you make it to my house on Saturday. We don't want you going and getting the Holy Ghost and then copping out," I said.

"I'll be there for sure; I want miss it for the world." he stated.

"Hey Keith, what did you do with Big Bubba when you took him home last week, was he big as the rumors?" I asked.

"Yes indeed, that sucker was 31 1/2 inches long and a little over 25lbs. My daddy took him to Haney's Sport & Goods to put him on a plaque." He replied.

"Oh, he took it to a taxidermy," Paul stated.

 "No dummy! He drove it to Haney's himself; he didn't use a taxi!"

"I'm in the seventh grade and even I know what a taxidermy is. That's when they put stuff on the inside to make it look like it's alive, just like them deer heads hanging from the wall at the Haney's Mart." Bobby explained.

"Shoo…, There's no way he would have been on a plaque. Big Bubba would have been on a plate with some good ole hot sauce, baked beans, and coleslaw." I said.

"Yeah…, that's the kind of stuff white folks do. There's no way that black folk's is going to let a 25-

pound fish make it past the dinner table," Paul said.

We all started laughing.

At this time, we began to hear loud stomach growls coming from Paul's stomach.

 "Dang…, now I'm hungry. I'm ready to go home and eat me some barbeque pig feet," Paul said.

"It's too hot out here to be eating pork!" Keith shouted.

"Well, I'm coming with you, because I'm getting sick and tired of eating chicken all the time. My momma cooks barbeque chicken, baked chicken, stewed chicken, and fried chicken; and makes chicken soup with all the leftovers at the end of each month" Bobby shouted.

"So that's why you be scared all the time.

They say you are what you eat." Keith jokingly stated.

We all started laughing again.

Well fellas, I hate to cut this visit short, but I have some final prepping to do between now and next week. See you at my house around 6:30, and make sure you are not on "BP" time." I said.

 "What is BP time, Bobby asked?"

"Black people time fool! You know black people ain't never on time!" I shouted.

2 Samuel 22:27

"With the pure, you will show yourself pure;

And with the devious, you will show yourself shrewd."

Chapter 4

*****

August 17, 1985

It was 11 a.m. on Saturday, and Momma had just gotten in from cleaning Mr. Haney's house.

"Steve!" she yelled.

"Huh?" I grunted.

"Boy..., you should a been at service last night, Jesus was in the building. We had folks come from all over. The church was so packed we had to start pulling out the folding chairs from the kitchen."

"How many people you think was there?" I inquired.

"It had to be over two thousand people in the church. They had folks from Jonesville and Waynesville County," she said.

"Are you telling me that those conceited folks from Jonesville came too?"

"Yes, those dignified folks were falling out all over the floor. When Bishop TC Collins started walking around with his cloth, he started swooshing people with it. Them dignified folks started falling out left and right. He even prophesized to Sister Mae and told her that its six things that God hate over in the book of Proverbs, and one verse came to mind concerning her.

Proverbs 6:19

A false witness who speaks lies and one who sows discord among brethren.

"He told her that God was not pleased, and she had to start humbling herself according to the word. You should have seen her face when Bishop hit her with the rag. She fell straight to the floor." she explained.

I didn't tell momma what Mrs. Mae had said in the store. I asked myself. How did Bishop TC Collins know that she was a gossiper. He must be a psychic.

"The Spirit was high in the church last night," she said while she was praising God.

"Did Bishop wear his brand-new fur coat?" I asked.

"Yes..., and you couldn't tell him nothing. That negro was "casket clean" in the pulpit. He even had armor barriers."

"Huh Ma, really?

"Yes, four of them too. He was in the pulpit trying to show off, and I guess he wanted to make sure that nobody would rob him of his mink fur coat," she said.

"In a Hundred and ten-degree weather? I think not!" I said.

We both laughed.

"Steve, James will be here around five o'clock later this evening to pick me up. We will be driving my car tonight because Mother Harris needs a ride to church. I need for you to clean out my back seat; to make room for her wheelchair."

"How come you not driving his car," I asked.

"James's car only has two doors; how are we supposed to get Mother Harris in and out of his car.

"Just do like I asked you to and stop asking so many questions!" She yelled.

"Yes ma'am," I said.

I began worrying about how we were going to move Annie. I knew that with the idea being mine: the boys weren't going to be so happy.

I had to rethink and maneuver my plans.

It was a little before five o'clock when I heard a knock at the door; it was James. He pulled up in his 1955 two-toned red and white Chevrolet Bel Air coupe that he won several years ago playing poker. He won it at a liquor house in Waynesville. I heard that he was one of the best poker players on the East Coast. James's car was in prestige condition except for a dent in the front right fender and a crack in the windshield.

"How's it going Steve, is your mother home?" he asked.

"Yeah," I said in a grumpy voice.

Momma came out of her room and realized that I left James on the front porch and didn't allow him to come in.

"Please forgive me James, Steve should have let you in. I apologize for his ignorance." She said.

I could tell from her devilish grin that she was furious. She always has that grin whenever she doesn't want others to know that she's mad.

I went straight to my room because I didn't want to be bothered with James. Every time he comes over, he always has this perverted look about him that always irks my nerves.

Momma finally left for church and didn't say "I love you" before leaving the house like she always does. I wanted to hurry up and get back home from Deadman's Curve to make sure that I was asleep whenever she got home. I knew that she was upset that I embarrassed her in front of company.

The time was 6:45 p.m., and I started to worry because I hadn't heard from the boys. I knew that they were probably confused because they didn't see my momma's car in the yard.

"Steve," I heard coming from the bushes.

"Is your mom home?" Keith whispered.

"No, she left a while ago," I replied.

"Man, we've been waiting on you for over twenty minutes," he said.

I explained the reason for the change in plans, and the backup plan was to use James's car instead. I went in the house, grabbed the bag of clothes for Annie, and after hot wiring James's car; we headed towards the school.

****

We finally made it to school and didn't realize how huge the suitcase was for Annie. Stealing James's car turned out to be a great idea after all. James's Bel Air had a huge trunk which made it convenient, but we had to remove the spare tire to fully close the trunk. As I started to lift the spare tire, I noticed a black wallet jammed in the left corner. I secretly placed the billfold in my pocket and placed the spare tire behind the bushes.

"Hey…, it's starting to rain. We need to hurry up and get to Deadman's Curve, because we have to give ourselves enough time to make sure that James's car is just like the way we found it." Paul said.

We slowly proceeded to Deadman's Curve.

" Slow down, I don't feel like dying tonight, and whatever you do, don't look into the rearview mirror. I don't want the ghost jumping out on us." Paul said.

"I see being a scaredy cat runs in the family." Keith said.

"I'm not scared; I hear growling sounds coming from the trunk," Paul explained.

"Growling sounds…, that's my stomach! " Bobby said.

We all laughed.

The rain stopped, so we pulled over and took Annie's suitcase from the trunk and placed it behind the big oak tree. We wanted to make sure that we had quick access to pulling her in and out of the curve. We opened the suitcase, stood her up and began dressing her with the clothes that I had in my black bag.
As I began dressing Annie, I looked over my right shoulder and a tear ran down my face. Looking at her brought back childhood memories of my grandmother.
"Steve, hurry up! We don't have all day. You are staring at Annie like you in love," teased Keith.
"Nobody's in love!" I yelled out of embarrassment. "I'm just making sure I didn't forget anything, that's all."

When we finished, we leaned Annie upright against the oak tree.
The air became silent as we all stared and looked at her for a few moments. None of us said anything,

but I knew that we were all thinking the same thing. My momma's dress and my granny's black veil made Annie look real. She had a heavenly glow that was so pure and radiant, it made her look like an Angel.

The car ride back to my house was full of excitement and anticipation. We were so amped; we unknowingly forgot to retrieve the spare tire that we hid behind the bushes.

Matthew 7:13

"Enter by the narrow gate; for wide is the gate and broad is the way that leads to destruction, and there are many who go in by it."

Chapter 5

*****

August 18, 1985

   It was Sunday morning and the big day that my friends and I had been waiting on for weeks. I knew that they too, were excited about scaring people on Deadman's Curve. I noticed that Momma was still asleep and was probably exhausted from the revival. Since it was women's day at the church, I wanted to surprise her with breakfast. Momma usually wakes me up with her cooking, so I wanted to return the favor.

The fire alarms were sounding, so momma was awakened from her sleep.
"What's burning," she hollered.
"Nothing ma, I'm cooking breakfast," I said.
"It looks like to me; you're trying to catch the house on fire. You don't suppose to cook with the stove set so high." She laughingly stated.
        The house was filled with smoke, while the fire alarms went off at the same time. I
        guess I didn't learn much from watching her cook over the years.

"What are you up to?" she asked. I know you're up to something, because I can feel it in my spirit."

"Nothing, I was just trying to do something nice for a change."

"I appreciate your intentions, but I'll take it from here. You know, I haven't had burnt bacon in years. I knew I should've bought you that Kiddie Bake oven set,'" she giggled.

"Kiddie Bake oven! Ma..., you trying to turn me into a Sissy?" I shouted.

"That's not nice Steve, just call it 'Free-spirited,'" she giggled as we both laughed.

Momma and I sat and begin eating the burnt breakfast that I had cooked. This was the first time in years that we sat down together at the dinner table and engaged in conversation. She started telling me about the revival and everyone that TC Collins had prophesized to. She started expressing her feeling towards everything from church, her life dreams, and her true feeling towards the Haney's. I never knew how much anger and hostility she had towards white people for the harsh treatment of colored folks.

I wanted to talk to her about my dad, but I knew that it would have changed the mood if I had mentioned anything about him. I really enjoyed our breakfast conversation.

After my breakfast with Momma, I went and started doing my chores. I didn't want her to find any excuse to try and keep me in the house. I had been excited all week and really didn't get much sleep these last couple of days. So, to stay focused and alert; I decided to take a nap.

"Steve!" Momma yelled.

"Huh ma?" I mumbled.

I jumped up and looked at the clock and realized that it was 5 o'clock.
"James is here to pick me up for church, I'll see you when I get back. I love you," she said.
I wanted to say I love you, but again, I couldn't get it out. The conversation we had earlier gave me a new sense of respect for her, but this childhood pride wouldn't let me say those three simple words. Thanks to our conversation earlier, I am now able to understand the reason why she does certain things.
The time was around 5:30, and I knew that I needed to start heading towards Deadman's Curve. I stay

on the north end of Haney County, so I knew that it would take me a little longer to get there then my friends.

I finally arrived at Deadman's Curve, and even though it wasn't quite dark yet, the rumors about the ghost had me nervous. I walked over towards the big oak tree to get a head start to scare my friends, but just as I proceeded in that direction, out from the sky jumped Annie. I screamed from the top of my lungs as loud as I could.
 Keith jumped from behind the tree laughing and yelled.

"I thought you were a tenor. Sounds like to me; you just hit a high 'E' note in second soprano. You scream just like "Antawn," that sissy choir director."

He started prancing around and singing the "E" note with both wrist limber in a female fashion.

"You play too much," I said.

"What did I tell you about the early bird? It always gets the worm?" he snickered.

 "Did you hook this up yourself?" I asked.

"Yes, it was easy and nothing but simple Physics. Once I created my fulcrum, all I had to do next was to figure out the load's weight to determine my effort."
At this point, Paul and Bobby jumped from behind the bushes.

Bobby shouted: "E=MC square "FOOL."

"E=MC square is Einsteins theory of relativity "dummy"!" Paul shouted.

We all started laughing.

Keith showed us how to maneuver and lower Annies body by using the pulley and lever technique idea that he stole from Archimedes. Then, we waited until it was completely dark because we wanted to scare one car at a time rather than those traveling in groups. That way, we could make sure that we had enough time to pull Annie's body back and hide her if we needed too. Once church let out, we knew that there would be a lot of people traveling home by using the shortcut through Deadman's Curve. We had Bobby sit a hundred yards north of the curve, while Paul sat a hundred yards south. They were the lookout guys that were going to let us know when cars were coming. We communicated with each other by using the handheld walkie-talkies that we generally used on our spy adventures.

The night was quiet, and it became very dark and gloomy. Then suddenly, Bobby radioed in to let us know that there was an incoming car headed our way.

 I got into position and lowered Annie onto the foggy curve. Immediately, you could hear the screeching sound of tires and a loud bang.

Someone just hit Annie.

I quickly pulled Annie back up and reeled her in to make sure that she was properly hid. The car stopped, and all you could hear were screams coming from the inside of the vehicle. The car sat there for a few minutes and then sped away. I recognized the car and realized that the car's screams and driver happen to be Mrs. Mae. When I realized that it was her, I found myself wishing the outcome was different. I was still angry at her because of our encounter at the store a couple of weeks prior.

We continued scaring people throughout the night, and we rotated to make sure that everyone had a chance to lower Annie's body onto the curve to see the reactions from drivers. We were able to scare a total of six drivers that night. We weren't sure whether people would report each incident, so

Keith thought it would be a good idea to put Annie back in her suitcase to keep her hidden; just in case the Sheriff's Department decided to investigate.

Proverbs 12:26

"The righteous should choose his friends carefully,
For the way of the wicked leads them astray".

Christopher B Howell

Chapter 6

*****

August 26, 1985

It was Monday and the first day of school. My friends and I had been going to Deadman's Curve every day for the last two weeks. Despite people running over Annie, we all noticed that there hadn't been any incidents reported to the local authorities. We took noticed that everyone that ran over Annie; all drove off without showing any concern. I must admit, I was really enjoying the excitement, especially after realizing that Mrs. Mae was my first victim. My friends and I were so excited about scaring people with Annie, that we forgot all about our favorite pastime of fishing.

"Steve," Keith said, "did you hear what happened to Mrs. Mae?"

"No, what happened to her?" I inquired.

"Her family had to put her in a crazy house last week. They say she's acting erratic. She's currently at the psych ward in Waynesville," he said.

"What happened to her," I asked.

"It had to happen when she ran over Annie two weeks ago. My mom told me she wrecked her car and hit her head on the windshield. They say the family can't tell what she hit," he said.

"Dang..., that's messed up," I replied.

"You are the man, Steve! You ran Mrs. Mae to the crazy house."

At that moment, I started feeling guilty and a little sorry for my actions. I noticed that Keith was getting a big kick out of the whole situation. He had a look on his face as if he wanted to try and outdo what I had done. I remained quiet for a moment while my friends kept ranting and raving about Deadman's Curve. Every time I tried to change the subject; they kept going on and on about the situation and commending me on a job well done.

The more they praised me, the more I truly began to feel sorrowful.

 I finally yelled aloud. "I'm getting sick and tired of talking about Annie and Deadman's curve. I'm not doing this anymore. I quit!"

"You ran an old lady to the crazy house, and now all of a sudden you want to start feeling guilty. I thought you didn't like her anyway," Keith shouted.

"Yeah Steve, Annie was your idea. You are the one who came up with the plan," Paul said.

"Yeah, but that was before I knew the things I know now."

"Before you knew what? You can leave, but Annie stays! If you try and take Annie or tell anybody about the plan, we will tell Mrs. Mae's family and the Sheriff what you did," Keith stated.

I looked at Bobby to see what kind of reaction I would get and hoped for his support. He just dropped his head and slowly began walking in the direction of Keith and Paul.

At that very moment, I knew that I'd just lost three of my closes' friends.

Mark 12:31

"And the second, like it, is this: 'You shall love your neighbor as yourself.' There is no other commandment greater than these."

Chapter 7

*****

October 21, 1985

It was Monday, October 21st, a week before the Inaugural Ball and my 16th birthday. Momma took the day off so that I could take the driver's test for my license. I knew that she didn't have a lot of money, so I asked her if I could use her car and take my test as my gift. She told me that if I passed, she would let me drive to the Inaugural ball next week and use her car for the remainder of the day.

"Steve, have you seen my black dress, I can't seem to find it." she asked.

"What black dress?" I asked, trying to avoid the question.

"My favorite one that you and James bought me for my birthday. I haven't had a chance to wear either one; now It seems I've lost the other."

I didn't want to lie to her, so I kept quiet while she remained puzzled. I knew it would break her heart if she knew that I dressed Annie with it. We finally left home, and momma dropped her dress off at the seamstress. This would be her first time wearing the dress, so she wanted it to fit perfectly for the County's inaugural fundraising Ball.

We made it to the DMV, and momma was shocked to find out that I passed my test on the first try. She didn't know that I had been sneaking and driving her car for the last two years while she slept. Momma held to her word, so I used her car for the rest of the day. I was excited about getting my license, but all I could think about for the last month was Mrs. Mae. I still felt guilty and remorseful for the way I acted in the store and causing her to go insane. So, I drove up to Waynesville Psychiatric Hospital to apologize and see how she was doing. I also wanted to know if she would explain what she meant that day in the store. I was curious to find out any information that I could concerning my father.

When I arrived at the hospital, I went inside and could barely recognize Mrs. Mae because she looked different from the way I remembered her. She looked much older and lost a significant amount of weight. The nurse stated that she had been unresponsive since her admission to the hospital. My granny always taught me that God judges you on how you treat others, not how others treat you. So...., I had to make peace with my soul.

I held her hand and introduced myself. I began to slowly speak and began apologizing for my behavior in the store. I grabbed the bible that laid on the floor and began reading her scriptures.

I questioned myself and wondered why did I come, especially after knowing that she wasn't responsive?

All she would do is just stare at the padded walls.

Then..., I remembered the words that I would say to my momma that would always comfort her in times of trouble. I held Mrs. Mae's hand and slowly whispered in her ear.

"Please forgive me?"

When I spoke those three simple words, a single tear ran down her face.

Christopher B Howell

1 John 4:1

"Beloved, believe not every spirit, but try the spirits whether they are of God: because many false prophets are gone out into the world."

Chapter 8

*****

October 28, 1985

It was Monday, October 28, and the day of the County's Inaugural Ball. I was still in grief because I found out that Mrs. Mae died only a few hours after my visit with her last week. She only had a few people that attended her funeral because of the gossip and rumors that she spread over the years. Many people believe that her condition was a curse from God ever since Bishop TC Collins prophesized to her that night at the revival. My friends and I were the only ones who knew the truth and the real reason why she was admitted into the insane asylum.

It had been weeks since my friends and I started scaring people on Deadman's Curve. Since then, there had been two reported deaths, and over two dozen injured. The rumors began to escalate because most of the ones who died, were those who received prophecy from Bishop TC Collins. The deaths had people from every county afraid to travel and use the shortcut from Jonesville to Haney County. With today being the County's Inaugural Ball, I knew the boys would use this to try and scare the newcomers who weren't familiar with the rumors.

The time was about 5:13 p.m., and only a few hours until the County's Inaugural Ball. I used momma's car every day since I received my license because she was using James's car to drive him back and forth to the hospital. James's cataracts were getting worse, and it made it hard for him to see at night. Momma and I were supposed to pick him up in Jonesville so that we could all ride together to the Inaugural Ball.

"Steve!" Momma shouted. "I need you to pick up Suzie Jenkins and her mother and take them to the Inaugural Ball. By the time I pick up James, we won't have enough time to pick them up and make it to the Ball on time."
Momma never liked being late, and I could hear the frustration in her voice. It was that same voice that she always has whenever she was running late for either work or church. I heard momma in her room, mumbling and talking to herself. She does this to help control her anger.

"This is the biggest day of Mr. Haney's life, and Lord knows I can't afford to be late", she mumbled.

I knew that staying out of the way was the best thing that I could do.

"Steve!" Momma shouted again. "Please make sure you allow yourself enough time to pick up Suzie Jenkins and her mother so that you can make it there on time. We are supposed to be there no later than 7 o'clock," she reiterated.

"Yes ma'am," I replied.

I walked into the living room and noticed momma in her favorite dress. This was the prettiest I'd ever seen her. She wore a pearl necklace and bracelet to complement the dress that she waited over nine months to wear.

"Wow...Momma, you look like a black Cinderella. The only thing that you're missing is a pair of glass shoes," I said.

She smiled from ear to ear and then quickly tamped down her elation.

 "Boy, I ain't got time to be fooling with you. I'm already running late. Just make sure you get to that Ball on time. I love you," she said as she hurried out the door.

I was amazed to see how beautiful she looked. She rushed out of the house just when I was finally ready to tell her those three simple words. I began to think and realized, that I had been using the fact of not having a father in my life as an excuse to make mischief. I've had the blessing and honor to have a mother, who raised me in the church and taught me how to be a man over the years.

As I began to think to myself, I prayed to God and confessed to him my sins and repented of all the things I had done. I said the sinner's prayer, and accepted Jesus Christ in my life, and became a Christian. I began to praise his holy name aloud as I began preparing myself for the fundraiser.

The time was about 6:00 p.m., and I knew that I only had a few minutes to spare before it was time for me to leave my house and pick up Suzie and her mother. I grabbed my black bag of fishing clothes that I hadn't washed in months and decided to clean them. I dumped the bag of clothes on the ground and looked down to find the wallet that I found in James' car. It had fallen to the floor, so I picked it up, opened it, and immediately became furious as I burst into tears. Inside the wallet, I found cash, a social security card and a driver's license which read "John Richardson.".

I asked God in my prayers for a picture of my Father, and to know the reason why he didn't come home that night. I new that with half of the prophecy revealed, I had to confront James and find out what happened to my father; and for him to explain the reason why my dad's wallet ended up in the trunk of his car.

My childhood anger resurfaced, I began to get furious and full of rage. My new acceptance of Christ in my life, and all those anger management classes, had no relevance. I needed an explanation from James to why my daddy never made it home that night. I began punching the walls with my fist and started throwing things across the room. I glanced at the clock and realized that I still had time to meet momma at James's house to openly confront him. If I took Deadman's Curve, I knew that we should make it to James' house around the same time. I jumped in momma's car and sped off as fast as I could, crying and beating my fist against the steering wheel. Once I arrived, I pulled up and stopped the vehicle about one hundred yards shy of the curve. I wanted the fellas to know that it was me. I told myself that I would put an end to this madness. My intensions were to take my ten years of frustration, loneliness and anger out on Annie. I grabbed my rearview mirror with both hands and stared for a moment, hoping to see the ghost. Instead, I saw the silhouette of my grandmother " Mrs. Annie Mae Stevenson," sitting in the back seat and looking like an Angel. I kept hearing her sweet voice steadily trying to whisper in my ear:

Romans 12:19

 "Beloved, do not avenge yourselves, but rather give place to wrath; for it is written, Vengeance is Mine, I will repay," says the Lord.

I was so consumed with my childhood anger that I ignored my inner conscience. My friends never knew my motive behind setting up the mannequin on Deadman's Curve. I maliciously did it out of anger that I had stored over the years from losing my dad, and then my granny a few years later. They never knew the mannequin was a molded image and replica of my grandmother that was donated to the school for her contribution and sacrifices she made over the years in the community. After all these years, I can't believe they had my granny's molded image desecrated, by stuffing her in a closet. The more I thought of the situation, the angrier I became. I was mad at the Church, the community, and with God for everything. I revved the motor on the engine several times before screeching the tires on the car. I drove recklessly towards the curve with no regards for anyone. As I approached the foggy curve, there stood Annie. I drove fearlessly over her body. Finally..., I've found solitude, peace, and restitution for my soul. I jumped out of the car full of anger screaming the names of my friends. "Keith, Paul, Bobby, It's over!" I repeated.

As I walked towards the big oak tree, I felt satisfied to finally be able to put her away. I knew that this would be her last day regardless of the consequences. I snugged my hand around the handle and snatched the suitcase; and to my astonishment out dropped Annie. She was wearing my mother's favorite dress.

 I paused for the moment and realized that with Annie before me, I assumed it to be the infamous ghost that everyone had spoken of. I walked through the foggy night and noticed lights blinking up ahead. As I walked towards the lights, I saw a car with the trunk wide open. It was a 1955 red and white two-tone Chevrolet Bel Air sitting on the side of the road with the truck open. It had a flat tire. I slowly moved forward and noticed that it was my mommas lifeless body looking up towards heaven and laying in a pool of blood.

With tears in my eyes, I held her tightly.

Now...., after all these years. I was finally ready to tell her those three simple words.

I LOVE YOU!"

Epilogue

Romans 7:19-25

[19] For the good that I would I do not: but the evil which I would not, that I do.

[20] Now if I do that I would not, it is no more I that do it, but sin that dwelleth in me.

[21] I find then a law, that, when I would do good, evil is present with me.

[22] For I delight in the law of God after the inward man:

[23] But I see another law in my members, warring against the law of my mind, and bringing me into captivity to the law of sin which is in my members.

[24] O wretched man that I am! who shall deliver me from the body of this death?

[25] I thank God through Jesus Christ our Lord. So then with the mind I myself serve the law of God; but with the flesh the law of sin.

The Malevolence of Annie Mae

www.ingramcontent.com/pod-product-compliance
Lightning Source LLC
Chambersburg PA
CBHW070508130626
46555CB00003B/1209